MONSTERS
IN SPACE!

GALAXY ZACK

MONSTERS IN SPACE!

By Ray O'Ryan

Illustrated by Colin Jack

LITTLE SIMON
New York   London   Toronto   Sydney   New Delhi

LITTLE SIMON

An imprint of Simon & Schuster Children's Publishing Division
1230 Avenue of the Americas, New York, New York 10020
Copyright © 2013 by Simon & Schuster, Inc.
All rights reserved, including the right of reproduction
in whole or in part in any form.
LITTLE SIMON is a registered trademark of Simon & Schuster, Inc., and
associated colophon is a trademark of Simon & Schuster, Inc.
For information about special discounts for bulk purchases, please
contact Simon & Schuster Special Sales at 1-866-506-1949 or
business@simonandschuster.com.
The Simon & Schuster Speakers Bureau can bring authors to your
live event. For more information or to book an event contact the
Simon & Schuster Speakers Bureau at 1-866-248-3049 or visit our
website at www.simonspeakers.com.
Initial interior sketches by Andrew Murray
Designed by Nicholas Sciacca
Manufactured in the United States of America 0713 FFG
First Edition 1 2 3 4 5 6 7 8 9 10
Library of Congress Cataloging-in-Publication Data
O'Ryan, Ray.
Monsters in space! / by Ray O'Ryan ; illustrated by Colin
Jack. — 1st ed.
p. cm. — (Galaxy Zack ; [4])
Summary: Zack is shocked to find a large, purple,
five-eyed creature sitting in his place at school one
morning, but soon learns that he and the "monster"
have a lot in common.
ISBN 978-1-4424-6718-7 (pbk. : alk. paper)
ISBN 978-1-4424-6721-7 (hardcover : alk. paper)
ISBN 978-1-4424-6722-4 (ebook : alk. paper)
[1. Science fiction. 2. Human-alien encounters—
Fiction. 3. Monsters—Fiction. 4. Friendship—Fiction.]
I. Jack, Colin. II. Title.
PZ7.O7843Mo 2013
[E]—dc23
2012024864

CONTENTS

Chapter 1
Class Monster!

Zack Nelson raced through the front door of Sprockets Academy. He was late for school.

Zack had dozed off that morning after his alarm went off. Breakfast took longer than usual, and his dog, Luna, had insisted on a last-minute walk.

Zack dashed across the wide lobby and ran into a round opening in the wall. A door hissed shut and he took off. The clear round elevator looked more like a giant plastic ball. It sped through a tube going sideways. Then a few seconds later it stopped.

A door whooshed open, and Zack burst into his classroom. Everyone in the class was already in his or her usual seat. Zack ran toward his seat and suddenly stopped in his tracks.

There's someone in my seat! Zack thought. He looked closely. *No! Not someone, some-THING! A monster!*

A huge purple monster sat in his seat. The monster was at least four times as big as Zack. It was furry with green patches, and it had five eyes. Its floppy ears stuck out from its face.

I've got to save my class before the monster does something terrible, Zack thought. *But how?*

Zack spotted Drake Taylor. Ever since Zack and his family moved from

Earth to Nebulon, Drake had been his best new friend. Zack hurried to Drake's side.

"Drake! What is that thing doing here?" Zack whispered, pointing at the monster.

The monster yawned. Its mouth was filled with big, sharp teeth.

"What's it going to do to us?" Zack asked.

Drake gave Zack a puzzled look. Before Drake could reply, their teacher, Ms. Rudolph, came into the room.

"Okay, class, let's begin," she said.
"Please turn on your edu-screens.
Today we are going to continue our
study of the second age of Nebulon
history."

Zack stared at Ms. Rudolph in
disbelief.

Doesn't she see it? he wondered. *Isn't she afraid of the monster?*

Ms. Rudolph soon began her lesson.

Zack looked around at his classmates. They were all paying attention. No one seemed bothered by the fact that a big purple monster was right there in the room.

Zack slipped into an empty seat.

Ms. Rudolph continued the lesson.

What's wrong with everyone? Zack wondered. Why aren't they scared?

Chapter 2

Lunch Monster!

The class continued as if everything were normal. Ms. Rudolph and Zack's classmates went through the lesson like they did each day.

You would think that it was normal for there to be a monster in our class! Zack thought. He tried his best to concentrate. But all he could do was stare at the strange-looking creature in his seat.

Lunchtime finally came. Zack and Drake headed to the space bus, which took them from the classroom to the cafeteria. They sat down at a table to eat their lunch.

But before Zack could take

a bite of his nebu-nut-butter sandwich, he spotted the monster. It was sitting just two tables away!

The monster pulled out a sandwich. Yellow worms squiggled between the pieces of blue bread. The monster took a big bite of the worm sandwich.

Yuck! Zack thought. *That is so disgusting!*

"So what were you trying to tell me before?" asked Drake.

Zack grabbed Drake's arm and pointed to the big purple creature at the nearby table.

"There was a monster in our

classroom!" Zack whispered. "And nobody seemed to notice. Now it's right here in the cafeteria. And still nobody cares. No one is scared. Except me!"

Drake laughed. "That is not a monster, Zack," Drake explained. "In case you never noticed, there are lots of different kinds of people on Nebulon.

That kid is a Plexi. He is from the planet Plexus. It is not too far from Nebulon."

"What's he doing here?" Zack asked. He was still uneasy having that scary-looking thing right there in his school.

"Oh, right," Drake said. "You came in late so you missed it. He told us that he is visiting Nebulon. He will be sitting in our class for a few days."

Zack took a bite of his sandwich. He continued to stare at the Plexi.

"I've never seen a monster before," said Zack. "At least, not a real one. It's like my nightmares are coming true!"

"Hold on," said Drake. "He is not a monster. He is just a guy who looks different from you. After all, you and I do not look the same, right?"

Zack thought about this for a moment. He realized that Drake was right. Drake was a Nebulite. His head was more egg-shaped that Zack's. His arms were longer and hung down to his knees.

When Zack first met Drake, he
noticed these differences. But once
they became friends, Zack never even
thought about them.

"Yeah, Drake, but you're not huge
and purple and furry," Zack said, "and
you don't have five eyes."

"What is the difference, Zack?" Drake asked.

Zack leaned in close to his friend. "Uhh . . . you are not a monster," Zack whispered.

He looked over at the monster. The big purple creature took another bite from his slimy, squiggly, worm sandwich.

"Yuck!" said Zack.

Chapter 3

Monster . . . or Not?

Zack hurried home after school. He ran inside his house. Luna was waiting in the kitchen. She stood up on her back legs and licked Zack's face.

"Hi, girl. I missed you too!" Zack said, scratching Luna's head.

"Welcome home, Master Just Zack,"

said Ira. Ira was the Nelson family's Indoor Robotic Assistant. "Would you like a spudsy melonade?"

"Sure!" cried Zack.

A panel in the wall slid open. A robot arm popped out holding a glass of lime-colored, frosty, bubbling juice.

Zack took the glass and gulped down the juice. "Thanks, Ira. Spudsy melonade is grape!"

On Nebulon, kids said "grape" when they thought that something was really cool. Zack had lived on Nebulon for only a few months. But the planet was really starting to feel like home.

Zack's mom stepped into the kitchen. She had just come home from work. Mrs. Nelson owned a boutique that sold Earth clothing to the women of Nebulon.

"Hi, honey. How was school today?" she asked.

Zack was so excited to get home and see Luna that he had forgotten all about the monster in his class.

Until now.

"There was a monster in my class!" he said.

"Really?" replied his mom.

Zack could tell from her voice that she didn't believe him.

"Maybe you shouldn't be reading so many 3-D holo-comics," said Mom.

Zack loved reading the comics on Nebulon. Each page came to life. Superheroes, dinosaurs, monsters, and more battled it out in 3-D, right before his eyes.

"No, Mom, I'm being serious," said Zack. "He was big and purple. And he was furry and covered with green patches. He had five eyes and floppy ears."

"And what makes you think he's a monster, Zack?" asked Mom.

"I just told you," Zack said. He couldn't understand how his mom was missing the point. "He's big and purple and has five—"

"All that means is that he looks different from you," explained Mom. "Just because he's different doesn't mean he's a monster. Drake doesn't look like you. Is he a monster?"

"No, of course not, but—"

"There are lots of different kinds of people on Nebulon," continued Mom, "just

like there are lots of different kinds of people back on Earth. That doesn't make any of them monsters, does it?"

"Well, no. I guess not," said Zack. He scratched his head, feeling a bit confused.

"We can talk more about this later, if you'd like," suggested Mom. "Luna has been waiting for you all day. Why don't you two play outside?"

Zack ran out the door.

"Come on, Luna!" he called.

Luna raced after him.

Zack held up a small ball. It flashed orange, then blue, then red, then green.

"Ready, girl?" asked Zack. The flashing ball was Luna's favorite toy.

Yip! Yip! barked Luna.

"Go get it!" Zack tossed the ball across the yard. Luna took off after it.

As the ball spun through the air, its many colors blended together.

Zack thought hard about what his mom had said.

Chapter 4
A Zandy Friend

The next day, Zack was on time for school. He walked into the classroom with his schoolmates. There, sitting in his seat again, was the monster.

"Okay, everyone take your seats," Ms. Rudolph announced. "Boys and girls, once again we have a guest in our classroom." Then she pointed right at the monster.

The monster stood slowly. He was even bigger than Zack had remembered. He walked to the front of the class and stood next to the teacher. The monster was twice as tall as Ms. Rudolph!

"I'm sure you may remember him from yesterday," said Ms. Rudolph.

Remember? thought Zack. *I haven't been able to think about anything else!*

"Today I want you to pay attention while he tells us a little bit about himself," Ms. Rudolph said.

The monster looked around the class. Then he smiled, showing off his big, sharp teeth.

"Hi, everyone," said the monster. "My name is Al."

Al? thought Zack. *That's a pretty friendly name for a monster.*

"My dad is here on Nebulon for a business trip. It's only for a week, but I came along because I really like this planet," explained Al.

Zack was amazed. Al's voice was soft and gentle. It wasn't the loud, deep, scary voice Zack remembered from monster movies he saw on Earth. In fact, Zack realized that Al sounded a lot like . . . well, a lot like him!

Zack thought again about what his mom had said. He remembered how worried he was when he first moved to Nebulon. Zack had thought the kids wouldn't like him because he was different from them. He recalled how happy he was that Drake sat next to him on the bus and wanted to be his friend.

Al took his seat again and Ms. Rudolph began the day's lessons.

When the bell rang for lunch, Zack and Drake hurried to the space bus. Zack saw that Al was sitting by himself.

Zack and Drake sat in the seat across from Al.

"Hey, Al! I'm Zack, and this is my friend Drake," Zack said. "Do you want to eat lunch with us today?"

Al's five eyes opened wide. He smiled. This time, Zack didn't even notice Al's teeth.

"Sure!" said Al.

"So what kind of business trip is your dad on?" asked Zack. Now that he realized that Al really wasn't a monster, he wanted to know more about him.

"He's a salesman," Al explained, "and I get to travel with him all over the universe. We're here because he wants to sell something at that place called—uh, what's it called?"

Al scratched his furry purple head as he thought. His ears spun around.

"Nebulonics! That's it," Al said. "A company called Nebulonics."

"My dad works at Nebulonics!" Zack cried.

I actually have something in common with Al! Zack thought. *Who would have thought?*

Zack smiled. "So I bet you've been to all the planets?" he asked excitedly.

"Well, not all of them," Al said. "There are so many planets to see! But we've been to quite a few. Good thing I love to travel in space."

"Me too!" exclaimed Zack. "My

favorite thing to do is planet hop!"

So we *have* a *lot in common!* Zack thought. *Just like we were friends.*

"My dad and I are going home this weekend to Plexus," said Al. "Would you and Drake like to come with us?"

"We sure would!" Drake and Zack shouted together.

"But we'll need to ask our parents first," said Zack. "We'll talk to them when we get home."

"Zandy!" said Al.

"'Zandy'?" asked Zack.

"What is 'zandy'?" Drake asked.

"That's what we say on Plexus when we think something is really, really great," explained Al.

"Grape!" said Zack.

"Cool!" added Drake.

Chapter 5

Plexus, Here We Come!

After school, Zack raced home. He dashed into his house.

"Mom!" he called out. "Mom, where are you?"

"Your mother is in the gym, Master Just Zack," explained Ira.

"Thanks, Ira," said Zack.

Zack hurried to the exercise room. He found his mother working out.

"Hi, Zack," said Mom. "Is everything okay?"

"Mom, remember that monster I told you about at school?" Zack asked.

"Well, honey, I told you that—"

"He's not really a monster," Zack

interrupted. "He's my new friend."

"That's wonderful, Zack," Mom said. "I'm very proud of you."

"His name is Al, and he asked me to visit his home planet for the weekend. His family will be there. And Al also asked Drake. Can I go? Please? Drake is asking his parents too."

"Dad and I can set up a video chat with Al's parents and Drake's parents," suggested Mom. "We can all meet— kind of—and make the arrangements."

"That is so grape, Mom!" cried Zack. "Al's dad is here working with Nebulonics. Maybe Dad already knows him."

Following dinner that evening, Zack's mom and dad settled down in front of the eight-foot-wide sonic cell monitor in their family room. A box popped up on the screen. The faces of Mr. and Mrs. Taylor, Drake's parents, appeared inside.

58

Zack peeked around the corner from the next room and watched silently.

"Nice to see you again," Mom said. "I'm so glad Zack and Drake have become such good friends. Drake has really helped him feel more at home here on Nebulon."

"And Drake thinks that Zack is . . ." Mrs. Taylor turned to her husband. "What is that word the kids like to use?"

"Grape," replied Mr. Taylor.

"Yes, grape," Mrs. Taylor said. "Drake thinks Zack is grape."

Zack covered his mouth so his parents wouldn't hear him giggle. Just hearing a grown-up use the word "grape" made him laugh.

At that moment two more boxes popped up on the big screen. Each box was filled with a big purple face. Each face had five eyes and two floppy ears and were covered in long, fluffy purple fur.

"I am Gur, father of Al," said one face.

"I am Toka, mother of Al," said the other face.

The other four parents introduced themselves too.

Through the monitor, Toka looked right at Zack's mom. She suddenly jumped back slightly.

"Are you all right, Toka?" Mom asked.

"My apologies," Toka said to Mom. "I was startled by how you look. You are . . . so . . . so different from those of us on Plexus."

Zack was amazed. *My mom looks so normal*, he thought.

"Hi, Gur. It's Otto Nelson," Dad said. "We met at Nebulonics today."

"Yes, we did," said Gur. "Our son, Al, would like to invite Zack and Drake to Plexus this weekend. We are so happy Al has made new friends so quickly."

"Yes," added Toka. "We travel to many planets. This may sound strange, but on some planets people are afraid of us. They think we look like . . . like monsters."

"We have met nice people from many worlds who live here on Nebulon," Mom explained, "and we would be happy to have Zack visit you on Plexus."

"We feel the same way about Drake," said Mrs. Taylor.

YES!!! thought Zack. *I'm going to Plexus!*

Chapter 6
Travel Time!

For the rest of the week all Zack could think about was his trip to Plexus. On Friday he made a list of the things he wanted to bring. He didn't want to forget anything important.

Let's see, he thought while sitting in math class. *Camtram, hyperphone,*

snacks for the ride, pictures of Nebulon and Earth to show Al and his parents.

Later that night as he drifted off to sleep, Zack imagined all the things he would see on Plexus.

The next morning, Zack, his parents, and his twin sisters, Charlotte and Cathy, went to the Creston City Spaceport. There, they met up with Drake and his parents, and Al and his dad.

"Is everyone ready for a fun weekend?" asked Gur.

"You bet, mister . . . uh . . . uh . . . ," Zack replied. "I'm sorry, I don't know Al's last name."

"We Plexi have only one name," Gur explained. "Please call me Gur."

"I have never been to Plexus," said Drake. "I cannot wait to see it."

"Then let's go!" said Gur.

The three boys walked up the steps to the space cruiser.

"Have a . . ."

". . . fun trip . . ."

". . . and take lots of . . ."

". . . pictures," said Charlotte and Cathy.

"Be careful!" Zack's mom said.

"And send me a z-mail when you get there," added Drake's mom.

Zack and the others stepped on board the space cruiser. A few minutes later, they were on their way to Plexus!

Chapter 7
A Whole New World

The space cruiser sped through the galaxy. Zack settled back in his seat and stared out the window. Planets, stars, and swirling colorful clouds of space gas zipped past.

"I can't wait to show you all the zandy stuff we have on Plexus," Al

said. "I'm happy we became friends so fast. You'll probably laugh at this, but I've been to some planets where they thought I was a monster! How silly is that?"

Zack thought about when he had first met Al. Then he laughed. "Yeah," he said. "Pretty silly."

A short time later the space cruiser began dropping down toward Plexus.

"Hang on, everybody," said Gur. "We'll be landing in a minute."

The first thing Zack noticed as they lowered down through the atmosphere was that Plexus had a yellow sky.

"That's amazing!" said Zack. "I've never seen a yellow sky before!"

The space cruiser gently touched down. Zack grabbed his bag and followed Al and Gur into the spaceport.

Both Zack and Drake stared with their mouths wide open.

People of every size, shape, and color filled the spaceport. Some were huge and covered with thick fur. Others walked on eight legs and made squeaking noises when they spoke. Some had three eyes that hung from their faces on long stalks.

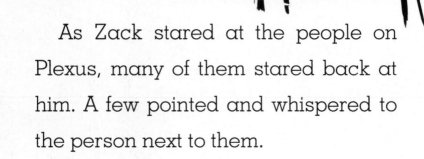

As Zack stared at the people on Plexus, many of them stared back at him. A few pointed and whispered to the person next to them.

Zack thought about how Al's mom had reacted when she first saw his mom. *I have to remember that I look as different to them as they do to me.*

"Come on, guys!" Al said laughing after a couple of minutes. "Don't just stand there staring. I have a lot to show you!"

Zack and Drake followed Al and Gur to their car. It looked more like a sleek space capsule. Everyone climbed in, and the car took off at super-high blinding speed.

"Wow!" said Zack. "Mr. Gur, you drive much faster on your

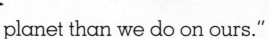

planet than we do on ours."

"Ha-ha—'Mr. Gur' sounds so unusual. Again, it's okay to just call me Gur. Don't worry; all cars on Plexus are controlled by computer-guided traffi-beams. They keep cars from crashing into one another—even at high speeds."

"Very zandy," said Zack.

A few minutes later they stopped in front of a box

that sat in a row of many other boxes. Each looked big enough to fit four or five people.

"Why are we stopping here?" Drake asked. "I thought we were going to your house."

"This *is* my house," said Al.

It's awfully small, thought Zack.

Al laughed. "Come on. I'll show you."

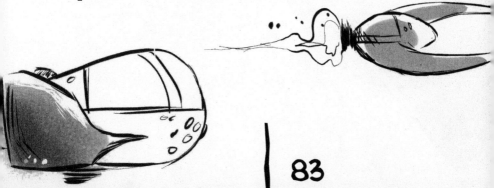

Chapter 8

Home, Sweet . . . Cave?

Zack, Drake, Al, and Gur all squeezed into the box. It began dropping down into the ground.

"It's an elevator!" said Zack.

"Yup," said Al. "My house is underground!"

The elevator stopped. Its door

whooshed open. Zack and the others
stepped into what looked like a huge
cave. The walls and ceiling were solid
rock. But this was no ordinary cave.

The entire house was filled with
high-tech gadgets. Zack recognized
most of them.

A robotic arm chopped and mixed food in the kitchen.

"I know that meal-o-matic," said Zack. "That was made at Nebulonics!"

"Most of this house has Nebulonics gadgets," explained Gur. "I have worked with them for many years."

"Welcome home, Gur. Welcome home, Al," said a voice that was very familiar to Zack.

"Ira?" Zack asked.

"Welcome, Zack Nelson. Welcome, Drake Taylor," said Ira.

"Yes," said Gur. "Our house came with an Indoor Robotic Assistant. That was invented at Nebulonics too."

Drake looked around. "You have the coolest house, Al," he said. "It is like living in a high-tech cave!"

"You haven't even seen my room yet!" exclaimed Al.

Al's mom walked into the room and gave Al a hug.

"Hi, Zack. Hi, Drake. I'm so glad you could visit," she said.

Zack and Drake both said hello to Toka.

"We're going to see my room," Al said.

Zack, Drake, and Al hurried down a stone hallway. They walked through a door at the end of the hall and into Al's room.

Zack spotted a computer screen that took up the entire wall.

"Pretty zandy, huh?" said Al. "I can watch movies, video chat with my friends from other planets, and look stuff up for school, all on this wall."

"Grape bed," Drake said, pointing

to a corner of the room. There, a bed hovered in midair.

"An antigravity beam holds it up," Al explained. "It lowers for me to get in and out. Then it floats while I sleep."

"Cool!" cried Zack.

Just then a window showing Al's mom appeared on the giant wall screen.

"Boys, it's time for lunch," she said.

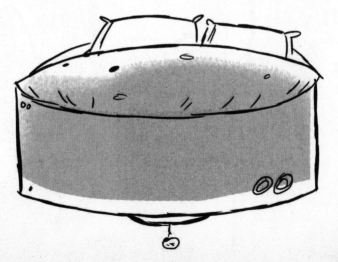

Chapter 9

Yummy Worms

Everyone piled back into the car. Soon they were on their way to a diner called Slime Time.

I wonder what the food will be like, Zack worried. *I remember that gross worm sandwich Al brought for lunch.*

Once they were seated in the diner,

a waiter with five arms walked past them. He carried a plate in each arm.

Cool, thought Zack. *I guess having that many arms would come in handy if you're a waiter.*

The waiter dropped off the food, then came over to their table. He handed everyone a menu.

Zack was nervous. Nothing he saw on the menu was the least bit familiar. The pictures all showed slimy, slithering food.

Does everyone on this planet eat worms? he wondered.

Then Al spoke up.

"Can we have three orders of twisty noods, please?" he asked.

"Twisty noods?" asked Drake. He was also worried about what to order. "What is that?"

"Oh, you'll see! They're delicious. I eat them in a sandwich at school sometimes," replied Al.

Oh no, Zack thought to himself in a panic. *They really ARE worms! What am I going to do? I can't eat WORMS!*

The waiter brought three plates and set them in front of the boys.

"These are twisty noods?" asked Zack. They looked like spaghetti.

"Mmm . . . ," said Al as he shoved a forkful into his mouth. "These are my favorite! Go ahead, try some!"

They smell pretty good, thought Zack. *And I AM pretty hungry.*

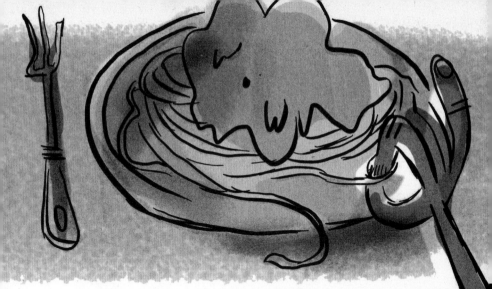

He took a bite. "Wow—these are delicious! They taste like chocolate-covered noodles!" said Zack.

"That's because they *are* chocolate-covered noodles!" exclaimed Al.

Not so strange after all, thought Zack. He gobbled down the rest of his twisty noods.

After lunch everyone went for a

short walk. They passed a park where a bunch of kids were playing a game. The kids were hitting a soft furry ball back and forth over an electronic net.

Al spotted a couple of his friends in the crowd.

"Hey, guys, these are my new

friends, Zack and Drake!" Al called out.

A short kid with arms that looked like snakes and one large eye in the middle of his stomach turned toward Al and his new friends.

"Monsters!" he cried, pointing at Zack and Drake.

"They're not monsters," replied Al. "They're zandy guys."

"But they look so . . . so . . . different!" said Al's friend.

"Nice to meet you," said Zack.

"Yeah, nice to meet you too," said Al's friend. "Sorry about calling you a monster. I just never saw anyone who looked like you."

"Same here," said Zack, smiling.

That evening Al's parents took the three boys to a movie called *Worm Blast!*

As the movie began, a robot arm popped from the seat and handed Zack a snack.

"What's this?" Zack whispered to Al.

"It's brick bark," Al whispered back.

"It's chocolate and plexu-nuts."

"Thanks," said Zack. He missed

popcorn but enjoyed the tasty treat.

Up on the screen, a giant worm exploded from the ground. Zack felt his seat shake. It felt like the action on the screen was really happening to him!

This so grape! he thought. *Going to the movies on Plexus is . . .*

zandy!

Back at Al's house, the boys looked at the pictures and videos Zack had taken that day with his camtram.

"I can't wait to show this to Bert," said Zack.

"Who's Bert?" asked Al.

"Bert is my friend from Earth," Zack explained. "That's where I was born."

Soon the boys grew sleepy. They were exhausted from their day.

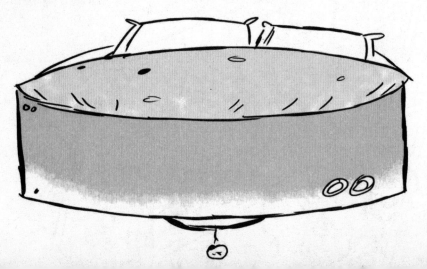

Chapter 10

Good-Bye, Friend

The next morning Zack, Drake, Al, and Gur piled into the space shooter and headed back to Nebulon. Zack arrived home and told his family all about his adventures on Plexus.

"Sounds like . . ."

". . . you made . . ."

". . . a good new friend," said Charlotte and Cathy.

"I sure did," said Zack. "And I learned some things too. It doesn't matter what someone *looks* like. What matters is who they are inside."

Zack's mom gave him a great big hug.

After school the next day Al came to Zack's house. As soon as he spotted Luna, he hid behind a counter.

"What's that?" asked Al, pointing at Luna.

"Don't be scared," said Zack. "Luna's my dog. She's very friendly. Pet her. . . . You'll see."

Al approached Luna slowly.

"I've never seen anything like her," he explained.

Al bent down and petted Luna gently on her head. She wagged her tail happily.

"See? She likes you!" said Zack.

Al smiled. Then he remembered why he had come over.

"My dad and I have to go home tomorrow,"

Al said, "but I hope we'll be back soon. . . ."

Zack started to feel sad. He remembered how he felt when he had to leave Earth . . . when he had to say goodbye to Bert.

"I had a really great time here on Nebulon," said Al.

"And I had a fun time on Plexus," replied Zack. "Let's video chat soon."

"Sounds zandy," said Al. "Bye."

Once Al had left, Zack headed to his room. He flopped onto his bed. He was

still feeling sad when the viewscreen in his bedroom began to blink.

"You have an incoming vid-mez, Master Just Zack," Ira announced.

Zack bounced from his bed and touched the screen. A box opened showing a picture of Bert and a message.

Zack listened to Bert's voice: "Hi, Zack. Guess what! I'm coming to visit you on Nebulon!"

"No WAAAAAY!" cried Zack. He couldn't be more excited.

I can't wait to show him all the zandy . . . I mean grape . . . I mean cool stuff on Nebulon!

GALAXY ZACK

ADVENTURE!

HERE'S A SNEAK PEEK!

Zack Nelson jumped up from his seat at the kitchen table. He had hardly taken a bite from the stack of nebu-cakes that sat on his plate.

"I can't believe he's coming today!" Zack cried. He threw both his arms into the air. Then he spun around in a circle and shouted, "YIPPEE WAH-WAH!"

"Honey, I know you're excited that Bert is coming to visit," said Shelly Nelson, Zack's mom. "But you haven't touched any of your breakfast. And it's almost time to leave for school."

"But *Bert* is coming!" Zack shouted. "I haven't seen him in so long!"

Bert Jones was Zack's best friend on Earth. Zack had not seen Bert since Zack and his family moved to Nebulon.

Zack missed Bert. And now Bert was coming from Earth to visit him on Nebulon. Zack couldn't wait to show Bert around his new home planet.

An excerpt from *Three's a Crowd!*

"Come on, honey. You have to eat something!" Mom insisted.

Zack leaned over his plate. He grabbed an entire nebu-cake and shoved it into his mouth.

"Dmvrum barimden," he mumbled through a mouthful of food.

"Don't talk with your mouth full," said Mom.

Zack swallowed and said, "Gotta go. Bye, Mom!"

"Have a good day at school," Mom said.

Now all I have to do is make it through the school day! Zack thought.

An excerpt from *Three's a Crowd!*